Forest of Memory

Also by Mary Robinette Kowal

FOREST OF MEMORY

MARY ROBINETTE KOWAL

A TOM DOHERTY ASSOCIATES BOOK
NEW YORK

FOREST OF MEMORY

Cover art by Victo Ngai
Cover design by Christine Foltzer

Edited by Lee Harris

A Tor Book
Published by Tom Doherty Associates, LLC
175 Fifth Avenue
New York, NY 10010

www.tor.com

Tor® is a registered trademark of Tom Doherty Associates, LLC

ISBN 978-0-7653-8389-1 (ebook)
ISBN 978-0-7653-8791-2 (trade paperback)

Originally published as an audio book by Audible as part of
METAtropolis: Green Space

First Tor Edition: March 2016

For Jay Lake and Ken Scholes
Who asked me to tell them a story

Forest of Memory

My name is Katya Gould. As you've requested, to guarantee this is a unique document, I'm typing it on the 1918 Corona 3 typewriter that I had in my bicycle cart when I was abducted by the man known as Johnny. You will receive both these pages and the tyepwriter.

And all of the typos that accompany this account.

The ribbon, incidentally, is a reproduction fab-matter ribbon. My habit, when I take on a new client, is to learn what I can of them, so that I can tailor my offerings to their tastes. About you, I know nothing beyond the fact that your payment cleared.

You might be a single person, or a collective artificial consciousness, or a cryptid represented by an avatar. I do not know if you have requested this document to solidify the provenance of your typewriter, or if you are interested in the possible connection between my abduction and the deer die-off, or if there is some other rationale behind your request, and so I hope you will forgive me if I do not write exactly what you have paid for. I am used to providing unique experiences or items to my clients, not to being one of those items.

On the seventh of April, I biked out to a vineyard in the Willamette Valley. In one of my standard datacrawls through public LiveConnects, Lizzie—

That's my intelligent system. I don't know what you call your i-Sys, but mine is named after a character in a book. I gave her the crisp diction of the long-vanished mid-Atlantic.

I'm an Authenticities dealer. This will hardly be my only eccentricity, and I will try not to digress further. So . . .

Anyway. Lizzie had flagged a possible typewriter. It was part of a display, and it was hard to tell if it was a re-pro printed with fab-matter or a genuine artifact. That's why you have to go see these things in person.

I wandered into the tasiting room, and the man behind the counter gave me a smile that almost looked genuine. "I'm pouring a couple of idfferent windes today." He set a glass on the counter. "What can I start you with?"

"Actually, I'm interested in part of your display." I pulled out a paper busineess card. That was Lizzie's cue to sned him my contact information. In return I got a data packet that identified him as Autrey Wesselman.

Wesselman took the business card, rubbing his thumb across the letterpress impression as he gave a low whistle. "Haven't seen one of these since my mom was running the place."

"Well, when you deal in Authenticities, an actual business card just seems appropriate."

He snorted. "If someone wants an authentic crappy fork lift, I've got one available. Guaranteed to stall at the least convenient moment."

"If you're serious, I might be able to find a home for that." I rested my elbows on the clean pine counter. Dings and scars testified to its lifeime of service in this tasting room. Too bad it was built in. "But I'm actually hoping I can take a look at your typewriter."

His brows went up. "Typewriter?"

My heart beat a little faster at that. The surprise in his voice sounded as if he didn't even know he had one. "There's a display in the member barrel room"

"Huh." Wesselman folded his bar towel. "That's my niece's domain. I just handle the tasting room."

"May I speak with her, then?"

He shrugged. "She's out of town on a sales trip. I can take you back there." He set the towel down and put an old bell in the center of the counter.

It looked to be from the mid-twentieth century, though without picking it up or using my loupe, I couldn't confirm that. The fine dust caked into the grooves around the base seemed real enough, though. Most people who print fakes know enough to add dust to make it seem older, but they usually put it on too thickly and without regard for the use patterns of everyday objects.

A small blackboard on a miniature wire easel went next to it. "Ring for service. Making wine."

I raised my eyebrows. "So you're the winemaker?"

He glanced at the sign and shook his head, wincing a little. "It's the easiest explanation, but no—not anymore. My niece handles that now."

"And you just do the tasting room?"

He tapped the side of his nose. "Concussion. Severed my olfactory nerves."

"Oh. Oh, I—I am so sorry."

"Years ago." He turned and walked toward the glass double doors that led to the back of the winery. "Got enough back so food doesn't taste like cardboard anymore, but not enough to make wine."

"But enough to do the tasting room."

"That?" He paused to hold the door open for me, and a wave of dark fruit aromas billowed into the winery. "They all taste the same now. I just rely on memory to describe them to customers."

Memory.

It seems like such an unreliable thing. I am so ~~used~~ accustomed to using my i-Sys, Lizzie, to recall recorded memories for me, yet she can only do that for audio and visual memories. What I smelled, or tasted, or felt, is another story. And what I thought?

I can use the saved record to remind myself of these sensory details, but my thoughts change based on the new viewing. I re-examine and revise my perspectives.

And without a recording . . .

We live so little of our days without a LiveConnect to record it. And the three days you are asking about are among those. I wonder if, in part, what youa re intetersted in is the very fact that I have memories unemcumbered by a verified record.

The part I'm telling you now, of course, occurred while I was still on the Grid. I don't have to remember the winemaker's words; I ~~can just ask~~ just asked Lizzie to do playback for me.

As I type this, I can see the winemaker's faded red hair catch the light in the late afternoon sun as we leave the wine room.

I can hear the sound of our footsteps tapping in and out of sync as we cross the vast space of the winery proper. The way the industrial white walls frame the rounded wood barrels and the purple stains on the cement floor are all part of ~~the record~~ my LiveConnect record.

We walked to a lacquered-wood door set into one wall of the winery. It was made of reclaimed barrel staves, straightened in a steamer and polished so the stain of pinot noir gleamed under the cool LED lights.

The interior of the member barrel room was dimmer than the working winery. Each barrel lay in its own cradle with a the member's name branded into the head of the barrel. A long table and library chairs turned it inot part laboratory, part reading room.

As we entered, Lizzie spoke in my ear. "The south wall has the display."

I turned south, and the wall matched the image she'd spotted on a member's public LiveConnect. An alcove had been set into the wall—probably to hold an old-style television at some point in the past—and it was filled now with someon'es imagining of what an office might have looked like.

It was the sort of mishmash of eras that treated the entire twentieth century as if it was all one thing.

The typewriter (this Corona #3 from 1918) sat next to a cordless phone (Bell from the mid-eighties), and an office plaque that, by its font, probably came from the 1950s. A stack of floppy discs sat atop a Samsung printer from the late nineties. And . . . wonder of wonders—a battered paperback *Webster's Dictionary*.

I do remember that my hands itched to pick it up the moment I saw it. The angle of the image Lizzie had snagged didn't show the paperback; it was beautifully worn, as if someone had really used it.

Wesselman cocked his head and wandered over to the alcove. "Huh. That looks nice. Not that I'm surprised. Amy has good taste. Literally."

I can hear my own laugh on the recording, and I probably smiled. "And in more than one area, apparently. May I?"

He shrugged. "Sure."

I picked up the dictionary first. The pages were yellowed with age, but not brittle. I opened the cover, taking care not to add any of my own imprints to it, and stared. Three different names had been written inside.

David Autrey

Leopold Wesselman

Amy Casteel

I had heard those names in conjunction with the family. "Relatives?" I tilted the book so he could see.

He cocked his head. "Yeah . . . my great-grandfather, granddad, and Mom."

I thumbed through the pages, which carried a record of the past. "This is gorgeous."

Wesselman's brow crinkled. "What? Really?"

"My clients are most excited by wabi-sabi—" I paused as the confusion on his face deepened. "It's a Japanese term. Something that witnesses and records the graceful decay of life. See? Someone underlined 'autocratic.' The ink is the same green as Leopold Wesselman's name, so he probably did the underlining. It's a tiny peek into his thoughts."

"Huh."

I turned to page seventy-four. "That coffee stain tells us that they were probably staying up late working."

"Or reading it over breakfast."

"Exactly. The question is more interesting than the answer." I closed it and thumbed the rough punctures on the cover. "Teeth marks. Someone had a dog. The hints are what make it so intriguing. Each piece of wear shows a part of the lifecycle of the book."

"Terroir."

"Pardon?" I looked up and to the left. Lizzie tracked my eye motion and supplied the definition.

She whispered, "Terroir is the characteristic taste and flavor—"

Wesselman's answer overpowered hers and she trailed off. "It's the unique expression of the terrain on the wine. Clone a grapevine and plant it somewhere different and the grapes change. Then the weather in a particular year changes the expression still more, so every wine is unique. Well . . . without weather control."

I laughed with delight. "Yes! We deal in very much the same concept, but different expressions of authentic experience." I set the dictionary down and ran my finger over the platen of the typewriter. "My clients can print anything they want, so what they crave are things that are truly unique."

"How about the typewriter?" He gestured with his chin toward the machine.

"Do you know its history?"

"I thought that was your job."

Sighing, I picked up the typewriter without asking for permission. Even though I've handled them before, I remember being startled by how light the Corona 3 was compared to some of the desktop typewriters. "I can tell you if it's a real typewriter, and make some guesses about the sort of use it saw, but that's not the same as a full provenance."

"Well. It's not a family piece. It belonged to a friend of my grandfather's, but I don't know who owend it before that."

"Did they werite on it?" I set it on the big library table in a puddle of golden light. The enamel on the edges of the chassis ~~were~~ was worn where the folding mechanism had banged into it.

"Dunno. Before my time."

What I want, in a situation likke this, is a complete oral history of the object. If there is a receipt o f purchase, that's even better. I rarely get that.

And I have clients who don't need it. Some of them are interested in the machine tiself and less so in the story that comes with it.

You seem to want both.

Or perhaps something else entirely. I can offer you a time-stamped LiveConnect record of everything I experienced up until I went off the Grid. There seems to be no need to tell you about the chipped enamel on the chassis. You can see that, well enough. Do you care that the wear pattern on the percentage symbol likely means that a previous owner worked in accounting?

I think it most likely that what you want to know is how the typewriter relates to Johnny. So I am going to suit myself, since your wishes are opaque to me, and jump ahead to after I negotiated for the typewriter and dictionary, and began to ride home.

———————

One of the things I pick up when I'm on my shopping trips are Captures. You might have even bought one of mine. The one of the farmhouse in southern Oregon, where I found a nest of kittens in an old clothes dryer? The audio of their purring and tiny mews still gets mixed into dance scores, even after all this time. You should see what I got for the dryer itself, since after the Capture it had a popularity provenance to boot. Between Captures and Authenticities, I don't have to turk myself out with a lot of little freelance jobs.

Sometimes that unique record is an experience, like this.

I always keep my Lens on, even when I'm just cycling from our homestead into Salem to catch the train or a blimp, and I pay for extra bandwidth for high-rez Captures. After I haggled for the typewriter, I rode my bike through the woods on the narrow road that led from the vineyard toward Salem. This first part is visible on my LiveConnect.

It starts with me on my bike. My plan was to ride up to Salem, hauling my cart of Authenticities, and hook up with the high-speed rail at the node there, then take that the rest of the way into Portland. Lizzie whispered in my earbud, "Deer crossing. Please check your progress."

"What's the penalty charge?" I had a meeting to get to and could NOT waste time out here. I mean, protecting species was great and all, but there were times when I wished the online community didn't place quite so much importance on noninterference with natural habitats. Would the deer really freak out that much if I biked in front of them?

"One hundred and fifty vinos." Anticipating my next question—I do have her well trained—the i-Sys whispered. "It is a small herd with five registered individuals in their corporate entity. Estimated wait time is three minutes." The fine was almost as much as my co-op fees for a month, so I decided to wait. I figured I could make up the delay.

It's important to understand, through this next bit, that I didn't know that I was offline already or that I was talking to Lizzie's buffer on my inboard system.

None of the warning indicators went off to indicate that I'd lost connection to the net.

I doubt my own mind, at times.

I'll tell you that it's strange trying to remember without being able to pull up the recording and just look at it.

I keep turning those three days over in my head so that, in some ways, they're sharper than any other memory in my life. In other ways, I think I'm wearing the edges off the memory by looking at it so much.But perhaps that wearing away is a form of wabi-sabi.

I've wondered what he would have done if I hadn't waited. It feels like he wanted me there to bear witness, but maybe it was just an opportunity that presented itself because I stopped. If I hadn't, if I had biked on through, would I have known that this was a cusp point in my life? Probably not.

It makes you wonder, doesn't it, how many other cusp points you sail through in life without any awareness. Heck, maybe the decision to pay me to tell this story will be one for you. How would your life be different if you weren't sitting where you are, reading this?

Not that I was thinking any of this at the time. I was just calculating credits and transit time. Sighing, I slowed the bike, and the quiet hum of the electric motor faded, leaving only the whisper of wind through the trees. Birdsong punctuated the stillness as I waited. A twig cracked.

Seemingly without transition, the deer was by the road ahead of me. A single doe, who turned briefly to look down the leafy corridor at me, large brown eyes staring. Then she continued without concern onto the narrow track. After a moment, another emerged from the trees, then a third. I sat on the bike as five deer languidly crossed the road, their hides rippling as they set each long leg on the pavement. The TOCK-TOCK of their hooves made a percussion track under the birdsong. It was exactly the sort of thing that some audio mixologist would love.

I subvocalized to Lizzie, "Capture last five minutes from the cache and see if there's a buyer."

The cloud cities were especially hot for "authentic" earthbound soundscapes.

"Confirmed. I would recommend holding still for another two minutes of buffer. I can remove the sound of your bike from the earlier track, but the manipulation will show in the file, diminishing the value."

"Understood." I would have to really hustle to make

the train, but it seemed likely to be worth it. The tricky thing about Authentic Captures is that people can spot the manipulation of the files—or rather, intelligent systems can, which amounts to the same thing.

Just like with the Unique Objects that I acquire, people want a Capture that gives them an experience they can't have on their own. Watching a herd of deer cross the road . . . You could have that if you were willing to wait, or if you got lucky. The quiet of this moment, the fact that you could hear the deer's hooves on the pavement, the breeze . . . all of these were specific to that moment. With a little space, someone could loop it back so that the deer endlessly snuck out of the forest and crossed the road.

You watched that recording. You know the utter peace I am talking about.

And you also know the recording cuts off.

The way the image seems to just stop looks like a bad edit, but it's actually the point where the local cache finally fills. Mind you, if I'd known I'd been offline for the past ten minutes, I could have recorded at a lower resolution and kept going for hours.

I could have had footage of HIM.

But I saw only the deer, crossing the road under a canopy of green leaves.

Everything from here forward . . . All of this is what I experienced, but I have no recorded memories of it. I can't play back this episode in my life and report on what I saw. I have to try to remember . . .

Have you tried to do this? Have you turned off your Lens, turned off your i-Sys, stepped away from the cloud, and just tried to REMEMBER something? It's hard, and the memories are mutable.

The cloud is just there, all the time. You reach for it without thinking and assume it will be there.

I might have heard a noise first, of a branch breaking, but seeing the way he moved through the woods later, I don't think I did. Even if it was there, it had no meaning at the time.

My first real awareness of him was the gunshot. It's an intense memory. As fuzzy as everything else is, I very clearly remember the slap of sound, as if a firecracker had gone off next to my ear. One of the deer jerked and fell. The crack came again, and another fell, and—

In fact, let me backtrack and try to really describe this, since that's what you're paying me for. The first deer to fall was the lead buck. He was standing about twenty-five feet away and watching as the other deer crossed. I saw him jerk first, and I didn't hear the sound until after that.

He staggered and took a step toward me. When he fell, he was staring straight at me, as if it were my fault. The sound of his antlers hitting the pavement filled the space between gunshots. The second one came before the other deer really had a chance to react to the leader falling. The next was a doe standing with her back to me. She had started to turn back in the direction they had come. There was that incredible blast that I felt more than heard as the sound cracked through the trees. Her hindquarters crumpled first, and she dropped to the pavement. Her head bounced. I jumped, trying to get free of the bike, absolutely sure I would be shot next. My feet tangled against the pedals, and I went down in a heap. The trailer I had hooked to the back of the bike tipped a little, but it kept the bike from going all the way over. The pedal scraped along my shin. I pushed back, away from the bike, set to run into the woods. I'd managed to get to my knees when I froze.

A man was standing in the road.

I didn't see him walk out of the trees, but he must have been in motion after the first gunshot, while I was busy falling down. But there were two shots, so maybe he was just closer to the road than I thought. It seemed as if the gunshots should have come from far away, instead of being right there. The noise though. It's actually hard to remember the sound exactly. I think what I have is a memory of remembering the gunshot, you know? It's as though it were too loud and too painful to actually hold. The part of the memory that hasn't gone is the intensity of the sound and the visceral way I felt it in my chest.

But you want to know about the man.

He was dressed in digitall camouflage and, standing in the road, looked like something out of an old video game. My first impression was of his solidity, however. He inhabited the road as if he had always been there. The deer were gone, except the two he had shot. Under one arm he carried a gun.

I didn't know what it was at the time, but I've looked at a lot of pictures since. I think it was a Colt R5670 assault rifle, but my memmory might have been faulty when I was looking at images afterward. He was around six feet tall, with broad shoulders that had a slight stoop to them, as if he spent a lot of time crouching. He wore a mask.

Not like a comic book superhero's mask. This was more like a balaclava that left only his eyes visible. Beneath the cloth, it was impossible to tell much except that his visible skin was a deep tan, and that his eyes were the same dark brown as the deer.

~~Not~~ It wasn't visible to me right then, but I eventually learned that he also wore a blocker that corrupted the smart dust as he passsed through it, so he didn't show up. A man-shaped void passing through the world.

Again, at the time, I didn't even know I wasn't recording anything. I thought he was doing this entire thing in

front of the world. At any moment, I fully expected Lizzie
to speak in my ear and tell me the authorities were on
the way. The fact that she hadn't done so yet probablly
cuased me as much panic as anything else.

I twisted free of the bike and half fell back. I think I
said soemthing stupid, like "Don't hurt me."

He snorted, the air puffing the mask away from his
face for a moment.

"You know someone is coming, right? If you hurt me,
they'll know."

He turned his back, totally unconcerned with me,
and strode to the buck. "Might want to check your connection, hon."

THAT was the moment when I realized I was offline.
I subvocalized first, the way I've done my entire life.
"Lizzie?"

~~I had~~ There was a slight ringing in my ears from the
gunshots, but nothing else. Aloud, ignoring the way my
voice carried, I said, "Lizzie. Lizzie, answer me."

"You're offline." The man knelt by the buck and slung
a bag off his shoulder. ~~The gun~~ He laid the gun in front of
him, so it would only take one motion to pick it up and
point it at me.

I pressed my hand to my earbud, as i f that would
somehow, magically, make Lizzie audible. She had a ten-
minute buffer that synced with my local system; this nor-

mally dealt with signal drop. The idea that I'd been out of range for that long was slowly dawning on me, but I was mostly in denial. I tried triggering a datacloud, but nothing appeared. Moving from eye gestures, I pulled out my h-stick, to see if I had maybe damaged it when I fell, but the green ready light glowed on top. I unrolled its screen, and it was 404 out of luck. "No signal," it said.

I had been scared before, but now I could barely catch my breath. If I had been standing, I think my knees would have given out.

My throat closed, and I could hear the wheezing as I tried to draw in air. I was ALONE with this man. Have you experienced that? Even in the middle of the night, when I wake up, there's always someone to talk to. There's always a witness. Without someone watching, people could do anything, and I was standing ALONE in a forest with a man with a gun.

"What do you want with me?"

"Nohting. You were just here." He pulled out a small kit from his pack. It was blue, I think. It fit in the palm of his hand, so it was maybe abuot the size of a long-term UV storage battery or one of the mass-market paperbacks that I sell. He popped it open and pulled out an injector. "Just keep quiet while I'm working. Deal?"

I nodded, but I still wanted to ask questions. I think it was because I couldn't connect that the need to touch the web became s o desperate. I kept swiping the screen of the h-stick, trying to get it to connect. Everything else about it worked fine. I could open my gallery but not patch in from my Lens, so the problem was entirely external. The only time I use the h-stick to show images is if I'm sharing them with someone in a digitaly noisy environment. Otherwise, we're all watching it in projected virteo.

This felt disconnected and unreal.

So I started talking, trying to fill in the missing information. "What are you doing?"

By that point, he had slid the injector into the skin at the base of the buck's neck. He squeezed the trigger, and I flinched, but it only made a muffled click. He pulled it out, ejected the needle, and loaded another one. His movements were smooth, as if he'd done this hundreds of times before. He popped a fresh needle on. I could see it from where I was standing. It was thicker than the cannula they use for blood draws.

"You'll have to pay a fine for killing them. There might be jail time."

"I didn't kill them."

I could see now that they were only tranquilllized. Their breathing was slow and steady. The fur on the doe's back was ruffled, but there was no blood staining her hide. At least none that I could see. "Still, interfering with a herd will have a fine atta ched." I waited for my i-Sys to report what that was, but I only heard the wind hiss through the leaves in reply.

The injector clicked as he squeezed the trigger again. "Sweetheart, if I was worried about a fine, do you think I would be doing this?"

"I don't even know what you're doing."

He pulled teh injector out and looked levelly at me. "Do you really want me to answer that?"

I stared at the gun lying in front of him and drew back. The sunlight seemed colder than it had before, and I pulled my sleeves down over my arms even though it meant covering my UV filter tattoos. Powering devices was not high on my list of concerns right then. But I did want to know what he was doing, that was the thing. I wanted to know, very badly, why he had shot two deer—

"Would you have to kill me if you told me?" I meant it as a joke, but it sure as hell didn't sound that way. It sounded like a business question at a meeting in the middle of a path under an archway of trees.

He gathered up the discarded needles and put them back into the medkit. Quickly, he resealed it and tucked it once more into his bag. He didn't even pretend to think about the answer. He didn't feint toward his gun or bluster, he just packed up his supplies as if I weren't even there. I was that little of a hassle for him.

I think it ticked me off. I'm trying to remember why I thought this was a good idea, but I mostly just remember feeling deeply annoyed.

I stood up.

He eyed me through his mask, but that was about it. If he could ignore me, then I could do the same to him. I righted my bicycle and made sure the hitch to my trailer wa s solid. The canvas solar top was still secured, but I opened it anyway to look at the items I was taking into Portland to sell.

This part I remember clearlly, and I understand EX-ACTLY why I remember it so well. I know what I had in the cart, because I cataloged it later as part of the ephemera associated with this experience. I'll bet you're wondering why I was able to keep all of these items and still vanish for a week into the woods.

I was offfline for three days, but I was gone longer.

I should get back to the deer.

He said, "May as well make yourself comfortable." He stood up and watched me fussing with my cart.

"I thought you said I could leave."

"No, I didn't."

"But you—"

"I said I didn't want you for anyhting. Didn't say you could leave."

"But—but—" I sputtered like an idiot, starting and

discarding all manner of pleas for mercy.

He grinned. The mask hid it, but his eyes suddenly crinkled. "It's fine. You can leave. After."

"After what?"

"After I'm finished. I am NOT in the mood to have a visit from the authorities while I'm working."

I shook my head, the fear still crawling up my spine. "I'm not going to tell anyone."

"No?" He jerked his chin, hidden behind its mask, at my h-stick. "And you're holding that because . . . ?"

To be honest, I had not realized that I still had it out. I was running my finger over the surface, tabbing between screens as if I would find new information. I jerked my thumb off the surface and shoved the thing into my pocket. "I was just looking to see if I had a signal."

"You don't." He picked up the rifle, which was no less terrifying now that I knew it shot tranqs. They were designed to take down a deer. No telling what they would do to me. He wandered over to where I stood by my cart. "What're you hauling?"

"I deal in Authenticities. Antiques, mostly." It was not, I thought, the moment to mention that I dealt in Captures as well. I very much wanted to get out of this alive, and despite his assurances about the deer, I was less than confident in my survival odds.

"Let me see?" He walked over to me, and it's hard to

describe the way he seemed to get bigger as he came. This is one place where a Capture would not have shown you the emotional experience, even if you were tapping directly into my vitals. There was a power in his movement, as if he were holding the earth down as he walked, as if he were grounding the world instead of the other way around. Up close, he was older than I'd thought. Above the mask, his face was creased with wrinkles. His eyebrows had been dark once, but were bushy with wild gray hairs now. I could only see from the bridge of his nose to right above his eyes, but it was enough to tell that he was laughing at me.

"What?" I moved to stand between him and my cart, though if he had chalenged me on it, I would have ~~let him~~ given him the whole thing in exchange for letting me walk away. The move was the unconscious part of my brain wanting to protect its possessions, regardless of the danger. The rest of my brain was busily engaged in screaming RUN!, and the two conflicting impulses led me to just stand in front of him. Not threatening, not retreating.

"I'm curious, and we have some time before they wake up." His eyes crinkled again. "Maybe I'll buy something."

"These aren't for sale."

"No?"

For a brief moment, my brain was actually smart. "I'm making a delivery. To Portland. My client is expecting me."

He ~~paused~~ cocked his head then, and his eyes went vague, looking off to the side at a projected virteo that didn't even show up in the daylight as a glimmer. He grunted and shook his head. "Or you've just purchased them yourself. Well . . . Katya Gould. We apparently have more to discuss than I thought we did."

In any other circumstance, the fact that he knew my name would have been no big deal. Facial recognition flags people all the time, so you know who you're talking to and how they stand in rankings compared to you. When I meet with a new client, I know their purchase history and the name of their first pet. What made this terrifying was that *I* didn't have a connection. He did.

Something to discuss? That did NOT sound good. And what had he seen in that pause? Something about who I'd bought the typewriter from? My client list? I stalled, pretending that antiques were the only business he could possibly mean. I can't tell you if I was doing that as a strategy—to try to seem as if I wasn't a threat—or if it was just a panicked coping mechanism. I remember it both ways.

"You're a collector?"

That smirk again, just peeking above the cloth. "Indirectly."

"You make a habit of being vague, don't you?"

"I make a habit of not answering questions I don't need to." He tilted his head at the deer. "Case in point. You, on the other hand, are very good at tracking down the provenance of the objects you sell and, more important, you have a client list that interests us."

"I note you said 'us.'"

"Yes." He shrugged and gave me nothing past that. "So, you have a typewriter, I see." They turned up in costume dramas often enough that I wasn't surprised he could name it. Though I was surprised by his next sentence. "That's the one war correspondents liked, isn't it?"

"Hemingway had one." I almost swung straight into the sales pitch, I but managed to hold my tongue. "You were interested in my clients. I should point out that I maintain complete confidentiality. I never discuss price or purchased items with others."

That's the thing about being an Authenticities dealer. People who seek my services want a unique experience, and that means they often don't even want other people to know what they have. There are some people who won't share their purchases with their spouses.

"Where do you get ribbons for them?"

That startled me, but not too much. "I print them." Seeing the surprise on his face, above the mask, I felt like

I had to justify it. "I include the original ribbon, but even with re-inking, most are close to two hundred years old, and too fragile to use. If someone actually wants to use the typewriter, and some people do, then I have to give them a reproduction ribbon. I label them."

He just grunted and picked up the dictionary, which made me think he might have been a collector. Someone else would have gone for the typewriter, mistaking it as the most valuable item. But the dictionary had a solid provenance and was dripping with wabi-sabi.

He thumbed open the first few pages. "How much?"

"You can't afford it."

"Maybe my client can. How much?"

So I told him and watched his brows rise to vanish under the bottom edge of his hood. He rolled his eyes, and for a moment I thought he was making a face at the amount, but the telltale shimmer of a virteo projection sprang into bein g in front of him. He made a few eye gestures and then blinked twice to shut the field down. "The vinos are in your account. Not that you can check, but they are there."

"Won't that tell me who you are?" The words were out of my mouth before I could think them through. I mean, maybe he hadn't killed me because he'd thought I couldn't identify him with the mask and all. If I had just reminded him that he had made a mistake, it would be appallingly stupid.

It didn't seem to bother him at all though. If anything, he seemed to find the question amusing. His eyes crinkled in another grin. "No."

Which was a relief and deeply disturbing at the same time. I mean . . . being able to mask transaction identification was high-level stuff, from what I understood. I occasionally had clients try it, but . . . well. My i-Sys is very good.

The dictionary vanished into his kit. The movement, and I'm sure this was calculated, showed a handgun under his coat, and another clip for the big firearm, which almost certainly did not have tranquilizers in it. "You'll want to cover up the cart, now. In case of rain."

There hadn't been any rain in the forecast when I'd left this morning, but I didn't argue. The man had a gun, after all, even if he had just paid an ungodly sum for the dictionary. Or his clients had, whoever they were. I tugged the tarp back into place, zipping it down. When it was sealed, the cart could be submerged in water up to ten feet in depth and the seals would hold. There wasn't any real need for that, but it had seemed like a good investment to be certain wind and rain couldn't get in. Sometimes I dealt in paper ephemera like the dictionary. Clients wanted to see the graceful decay of age, not mishandling by their broker, which meant I had to be able to annnotate damage. Recent water damage? Didn't sell.

I had the cart half covered before my brain processed what he'd said and the red flag it raised. I was only an hour out of Salem, and the sky through teh trees was a crystal-clear blue. "There's no rain in the forecast today." Here's where Lizzie should have confirmed that for me, but my earbud remained stubbornly silent.

He stepped back, turning out a little so the deer came into his line of sight without his needing to turn his back on me. "We've got about twenty minutes before they wake up. Need to get the cart off the road."

"I'm not . . . I'm not—what are you going to do with me?"

"I want you to push the bike back the way you came. I'll be right behind you."

I shook my head and backed away from him. This was not going anywhere good. Turn my back on him? Walk away, with him standing behind me with a gun, and push the bike off the road? I didn't know why—or even IF—he'd paid for the fdictionary, but my brain put together this whole scenario where he was about to kill me and had framed someone else by using their account for the transfer. All he had to do was hide my body. Anyone watching my live feed would see where I disappeared from the net and would look forward for me first, along the route I'd been traveling. If I went backward, it would take them longer to find me.

And how long would it take someone to notice I was gone? Presumably, my i-Sys would be rasising flags right now, but I didn't actually know that. I mean . . . I didn't know anyone who'd been off the grid for more than a couple of minutes at a time, and that was always in places where the reception was known to be spotty. Spelunkers whose smart-dust trails were interrupted, things like that. Would my disappearance be remarked upon, or would it look like equipment failure? Or had he made arrangements to cover that, even?

He hadn't. I didn't know this then, but he was working with a ticking clock that had nothing to do with the deer. I'd been a minor bobble in his day; he'd been planning to release me, until his client changed his plans. My i-Sys WAS sending up all sorts of system flags and trying to arrange for a search-and-rescue team to look for me. All I knew at the time was panic.

I thought I would probably have better odds sprinting for the woods. At least the trees might make it harder for him to shoot me. That was why he'd waited until the deer were on the road, right?

He saw all of that and lifted the gun, just a little, so that it pointed more toward me. "Just put your hands on the handlebars and turn the bike around. Nice and slow."

I did. What I remember most clearly is the sweat running down the backs of my knees. That's a funny place for sweat, isn't it? You think about fear and clammmy palms, or sweat on your forehead, but it was my knees. I thought they would crumple with each step. I THINK he helped me turn the bike, because the path was so narrow that it would have been hard to do with the cart, but I don't remember for sure. I justr emember the backs of my knees tickling as sweat slid down from my thighs to my calves.

There wasn't anything realistic I could do, so I walked the bike, expectings omething to hit me from behind with each step. "How far do you want me to go?"

"Just keep walking."

"It'd be faster if I rode."

He snorted at that. I didn't look over my shoulder, even though he didn't tell me to keep staringstraight ahead—or at least, I don't think he did. All the scary movies I'd seen and the books I'd read over the years told me that looking back caused bad things to happen. After a while—I'm not sure how long, since I've discovered that I'm a crap judge of time without an i-Sys to remind me—he said, "Turn off here. To the right."

He put just enough pressure on the cart that I had to slow, and I think I was in enough shock that I just followed his command. I stepped off the road and followed his instructions as we pushed the bike through the woods and around clumps of ferns. The undergrowth slapped my legs with slender branches, leaving welts on my bare calves as if I'd been beaten with tiny switches. I envied the man's long trousers and shirt sleeves. Once he had to help me boost the bike and cart over a moss-covered log. He slung the rifle over his shoulder in order to use both hands to lift the cart.

In hindsight, I have this mental image of shoving the bike and trailer back toward him. It would have knocked him off balance. He might even have been pinned for a moment by the cart. I could have run into the woods and dropped behind one of the thickets, burrowed into the ferns and gotten away.

Instead, I thanked him for helping. I THANKED him. That still burns.

But it also snapped me out of the shock a little as I realized that I was just going along with whatever he wanted me to do. It's easy for you to sit there and wonder why I didn't try to escape, but by this point, maybe only ten minute s had passed. My mind was still trying to understand what had happened. I started looking for another opportunity. Started trying to think through what would happen if I ran. I kept subvocalizing questions to Lizzie, out of sheer reflex, and the continuing silence made me raelize how much I relied on her to help me make decisions. It wasn't so much that she told me what to do as that I liked having someone to bounce ideas off of. So don't judge me for taking ten minutes before I genuinely tried to think of ways to escape.

I've gotten a lot of flak for making this up, or for being a willling victim. I wasn't. And I can't prove that to anyone because there's no record. This was hard for me.

We went deeper still into the woods. Underneath the wind, I could just make out the sound of water running. It was the tantalizing sound of freedom.

He stopped and pointed at a small clump of saplings.

"Here. This is good."

He pulled the branches aside and gestured for me to push the bike and trailer back into the space. It did not take him long to drag underbrush up to mask my equipment. At first I thought it was not very well hidden, but the random branches and leaves he'd thrown over it broke the shape up enough that it was hard to spot, even knowing exactly where it was.

He told me to walk ahead of him and he tidied up the signs of our passage as we ~~walked back~~ returned to the road. When we got back to it, I was surprised by how far away we were from the deer.

The buck lifted his head, and the man swore.

"That took longer than I expected."

At first I thought he meant the drug had taken longer to wear off, but then I realized he was talking about hiding the bike.

He shook his head and ran past me to the deer, slinging his gun in front of him. His feet made no sound at all on the pavement. I watched him run for a minute as I continued walking forward, as if he were behind me and forcing me. Then my brain caught up with the fact that he was completely distracted. I stopped.

I don't remember really weighing the options. I just turned and slipped off the road back into the underbrush and headed toward the sound of the stream. I say "slipped" as if I were at all graceful, but compared to the man, I sounded like a demo team tearing up an old road. He slowed and glanced over his shoulder as I crashed through the leaves. I didn't care. I just barreled between the trees. By this point, I was thinking at least a little clearly, and I RAN, not caring about how big a path I tore through the woods. I figured that even if he saw me go, he still had to deal with the deer, and the more distance I put between us the harder it would be for him to find me when I went to ground. More important, there was a chance that if I left the range of his damper, my i-Sys could spot me again.

I was breaking branches, and I knew I'd be easy to track, but I had the sense that he would have found me easily even if I'd demonstrated impeccable woodcraft. I strained my ears to listen fo r him, but beyond the sound of bracken crackling underfoot and my own labored breathing, I couldn't make out the sound of anything else moving in the forest. The trickle of water came and went between my footfalls, and I just aimed toward where it was loudest.

I passed a mossy log with a gap under it that was just big enough for a person to hide in. I got this idea that I could make a false trail and double back to hide under it. So I ran on. The idea was that getting to the stream would make it harder to tell that my trail had vanished. In theory. I had read about it, and it certianly seemed to make logical sense, but I didn't know if that was a literary convention or if streams really were good tools for throwing someone off your scent. On the other hand, it wasn't as if he were going to be smelling my trail. At least, I didn't think he would.

The angle of the ground pitched down ahead of me, and I crested the top of a little hill. At the bottom was the stream I'd been running toward. It was narrow and had ferns crowding the sides. I slid down the bank and landed with a splash. Heart hammering, I stood in the rushing water and listened. The brook babbled around my ankles, but I heard nothing beyond the water.

"Lizzie?" I pressed my hand to my earbud. "Can you hear me?"

I didn't really think it was likely yet, and the silence confirmed that I was still in range of whatever he had used to block me. As carefully as I could, I pulled myself up out of the stream, trying not to make it obvious that I was backtracking. I tried to be quiet as I crept back along the path I had torn through the woods. My chest hurt because I kept trying to hold my breath so it didn't make any noise, hoping I could hear if he was coming toward me. He'd been so silent on the road. I tried to reassure myself that it had been the pavement. I'd heard him make noise as we walked in the woods with the bike, but not when he'd stepped out of the trees.

Clearly, he could be quiet when he needed to be. I tried placing my feet carefully, but even so the leaves rustled and shushed under me as if they were trying to warn me that I was too loud. I could hardly draw air. Every fiber in my body screamed at me to turn around and not walk toward him. I kept going, hoping I could convince him that I was running downstream. I heard crashing in the forest at some distance. I didn't think it could be him, the noise was so loud. The deer, I decided, had gotten to their feet, at least one of them, and were entering the woods. Was that good or bad?

I had no idea. Wit h luck, he was going to follow them. Without luck, that meant whatever he was doing was finished and he could focus on finding me. I was drenched in sweat by this point as the thermal battery fibers in my clothes utterly failed to keep up with the excess of panicked heat I was generating. Still, I kept going, not hearing anything. It seemed as if the distance from the stream back to the moss-covered log had lengthened while I'd been walking. Any moment, I was sure he would appear in front of me. When I reached the log, I stepped carefully over it, not disturbing the moss, and pushed in from the back into the little hollow beneath it. I shoved leaves in front of me to create a small blind, masking me from view if he was following my trail.

The ground was cool, and the leaves clung to my face. I remember being surprised by how damp it was. That was a relief at first, helping me cool down after my run. The spicy, almost cinnamon aroma of the crushed leaves was soothing as I lay there and waited. What I was hoping, desperately, was that he would either not look for me, or look and give up.

As I lay there, limbs stiffening in the embrace of the earth, I heard a low hum. The slight ticking of gears going around almost blended with the breeze. A bike was on the road. It did not slow as it went past. If I had stayed on the road, would that person have been able to save me? Just having someone else present might have been enough to get me away from him—but I had run into the woods.

The bike didn't slow, so I assumed the deer were gone. Now I just had to figure out how long I needed to wait to be certain he was gone as well.

My right hand started to fall asleep. Pins and needles prickled in the side of my palm, and I flexed my fingers, trying to keep the circulation going without making a sound.

A twig cracked. I stopped breathing for a moment, absolutely certain I had somehow broken the stick myself. The more horrible and totally obvious idea came next. Another person had broken the stick. He was tracking me. I closed my eyes, as if that would somehow make it harder to find me. In the waiting darkness, I focused on listening for sounds of him. A rustle that wasn't in time with the breeze. A squelch of a foot on soft leaves. Then a sigh.

It really is amazing how loud a sigh can sound in the forest.

"Come out from under the log, Katya."

I opened my eyes. With the leaves, I was in a cool, dark shelter of filtered green and brown. A childish part of me wanted to stay still, as if pretending I wasn't there would make him go away. It was all too clear that my flight down to the creek had not fooled him for a moment. "The cyclist will hear the rifle if you shoot me."

"That is correct."

And then he cocked the rifle. The sigh had been bad. The sound of that small, metallic click . . . It couldn't have echoed—we were in the woods, for crying out loud—but it still reverberates in my mind.

Now, clearly, I'm not dead. Clearly, I came out from under the log. Leaves clung to me. Mud and scratches covered my legs and arms. He stood there, his eyes blank above the mask. The rifle was pointed at my sternum. My memory breaks here.

I don't remember being shot.

I wish I could give you some poetic langauge about how things grew hazy or how I asked him "Why!?" in an impassioned tone, but that would be bullshit. It turns out that when you are drugged like that, there's a jump cut in your memory. One minute I was standing in the forest; the next, I was lying on my back in a tent.

Well . . . I say I was lying in a tent. It took me a minute to sort that out. Waking up was confusing. My head was too heavy to lift, and my eye s felt as if they had been filled with sand. I stared at the dappled cloth over me and couldn't figure out what it was. At first I thought the patterns on the ceiling were moving because I was drunk, but it was just the shadows of leaves. I don't know how much time passed as I drifted in and out of consciousness, surprised anew each time I awoke. The remnants of the drug kept trying to pull me back down into sleep. In fact, I'm not entirely certain that I didn't fall asleep again. I remember murmuring to ask Lizzie to keep me awake.

Her silence was baffling. Then, FINALLY, I remembered what had happened.

My eyes opened w ide at the memory of the man aiming the rifle at me. I lay there trying to listen for some sign of him and had to fight to avoid drifting off again. I pushed myself to a sitting position, the tent pitching around me. It was a small space with walls of a synthetic silk compound. He'd set it up between two trees, and the smart fabric had wraped itself around the trunks as additional supports, making something about the size of an old pup tent. The ceiling brushed my hair when I sat up. The interior was filled with the scent of my own sweat and the decay of my breath. The sides of the tent turned in spirals around me. I gripped the thin thermal blanket in both hands and held on until the space steadied.

There were so few things that made sense about the whole experience; I'm not sure why I expected events to suddenly appear orderly and rational now. Holding my head, I listened past the walls of the tent for someone else. I heard nothing, but that was proof of not a thing beyond the fact that he could be exceedingly quiet when he chose to be. For all I knew, he was standing just outside the tent and watching me.

I suppose I should backtrack here to explain that one of the things I noticed when I woke up was that someone had washed me, but that I was wearing the same clothes.

The thing I didn't know, and couldn't know, and still don't know was whether or not ~~anyone~~ he had undressed me in the process of cleaning the mud from my skin. It was a profoundly creepy thought. Really. I felt more unclean than when I'd had mud all over my body. Lizzie couldn't tell me. The only thing I had was the report of my own sensations, and they felt profoundly unreliable in that moment. I could barely turn my head without puking from dizziness.

What had the deer felt like when it had awoken? I mean, that rack of antlers must have pulled its head back down even more than my own wanted to droop. My first instinct was to crawl out of the tent and try to stagger away into the woods, but—let's face it—he had found me easily when I was in full possession of my senses. The smart course was to wait until the rest of the tranquilizer wore off before going out.

The tent flap opened.

I will admit: I jumped and gave a little squeal.

He was kneeling in the dried leaves outside the tent, still with that damned mask over his lower face. I hadn't heard him AT ALL.

He paused, watching me recover from being startled, and tilted his head. "How do you feel?"

"Bastard."

He didn't respond, just waited. I squinted past him,

but the light outside the dim interior of the tent dazzled my eyes almost to the point of pain. All I could really see was that we were still in a forest. I presumed it was the same one.

I was wrong, of course, but I wouldn't know that until later.

I still don't know how he moved me from a forest outside Salem to one in Washington. I mean, we must have been in a vehicle of some sort, but that's just one more giant gaping hole in my story. I only promised to tell you what I experienced though, so the things I didn't . . . well. You can't blame me for not knowing them, can you?

Anyway, he knelt there, waiting, and I sat there being stubbornly righteous and feeling as if answering any questions would be giving in to my captivity. He didn't seem particularly put out, but then it's sort of hard to tell what someone thinks when they have a full face mask on. He passed me a water bottle.

Or rather, he held one out, but I didn't take it. He shrugged and set it down on the floor of the tent. "You'll be thirsty. Drink it slowly."

Then he let the flap fall. I didn't hear him walk away, but I hadn't heard him approach the tent either. For all I knew he was right on the other side of the flap, waiting for me to move. It was incredibly maddening. Every breath I took seemed too loud. The air in the tent burned my throat. I put my hands to my head and bent forward, trying to get a grip on myself.

That's when I noticed, finally, that my earbud was gone. He must have taken it off while I was unconscious.

Which meant that maybe we were somewhere with net access. That gave me a little bit of hope. Not immediately, of course. No, first came yet another sense of being violated and panic about being disconnected. I pawed aside the sleeping roll I'd been on and pushed away everything in the tent, hoping my earbud had just fallen out. As if. The thing was custom molded to my ear canal and wouldn't even come out when I was swimming. Heck, I'd been surfing and gotten pounded by waves with it in.

No. The answer was that the man had taken it out. I sat in the mess of blankets, my head touching the ceiling of the tent, and slowly rebuilt my thoughts.

First: I wasn't dead. He'd taken the trouble to tranquilize me and bring me to Washington—well. I mean, at the time, it was still just "somewhere," but I wasn't dead. That meant I had some value, some usefulness to him.

Second: He'd taken the earbud, but he hadn't demanded it when we'd been on the road. That meant something was different about our environment. If I could get my hands on a network-enabled device, maybe I could get help.

Third: None of this was going to happen quickly, so I needed to drink the damn water.

You don't reall y think of taking charge of your physical needs as a big heroic thing, but at the moment, anything that was under my direct control was a lifeline. The lid cracked, and I remember being relieved that it was a sealed bottle, because that meant he wasn't trying to poison me. As if there weren't easier ways to do me in. Trust me, once you start having paranoid thoughts, everything becomes suspicious.

And yes, he was rihgt to warn me to drink it slowly. I was thirsty. Thirstier than I expected to be, which made me wonder how long I had been asleep.

I set the bottle down with half the water still in it and stared at the flap of the tent. He hadn't told me to stay in the tent, so I pushed the flap aside and crawled out. I had to squint my eyes nearly shut at first. I would have made a crap spy.

I stood up, staggering as my balance went all wonky. Inside the tent, my vision had stabilized, but getting to my feet brought all the symptoms of the tranquilizer back again. The trees spun around me in ways I had previously considered entirely metaphorical. Before I pitched over, he was at my side and had a hand under my elbow, another at the small of my back.

"Easy." He steadied me, not standing closer than was

necessary.

I stared at the ground, wanting to pull away, but knowing that any sudden movement would tip me over. When the ground wasn't moving quite so much, I released my breath. "Thank you."

With a quick squeeze of my arm, he nodded and stepped away. "Sorry about that. Sucks to wake up from."

"Why?"

To his credit, he could have misinterpreted that as a question about the effects of the drug, but he answered the question I had meant to ask. "You ran once already. I'm on a schedule."

"Running seemed reasonable at the time."

"I'll grant that it might have. Does it still?"

"It would help if I knew what you wanted with me."

"Not me, sweetheart. My bosses."

"The question still stands."

He grunted and walked away from me to a small camp chair. The low angle of the light cut under the branches and shone in my eyes. My vision had cleared some, but I still was having trouble focusing, so let me tell you about where we were based on a latrer memory. This one was full of fuzz and twisting shadows from the evening sun.

The real space was a clearing about ten meters wide. Large enough for the tent, fairly level, with light filtering down from the trees overhead. A passing airplane wouldn't spot us. He'd set up a small camp table with a chair in front of it. The table held a careful stack of supplies. It looked like a mix of electronic and medical equipment. The vaccination gun, tranquilizer darts, an external monitor, and an honest-to-god hard-body computer case.

Crouched on the ground, in deactivated mode, was a robo-mule, which must have been how he had carried all of this gear into the woods. It meant that we were probably not currently close to a road, and that a vehicle must have been used at some point to transport the robo-mule. Presumably me too.

The rifle leaned against the table.

He pulled the camp chair away from the table and set it down in the middle of the clearing. "Have a seat."

"Where will you sit?"

"Log." He jutted his chin toward a massive stump that was almost chair height and had the width of an ancient old-growth tree. It must have been a remnant of the old logging days. The top was a deep weathered brown and ha d a film of moss around the edges. "Hungry?"

Again, the urge to say no pressed at my lips, but really . . . was I worried it might not be safe? Or that I would betray some principle by not accepting his food? The only person I would hurt was me, and I would need my strength. So I accepted.

He nodded, pleased by my response, and that nearly made me change my mind. But it occurred to me that if he ate with me, he'd have to take the mask off. I crosssed to the camp chair, still a little unsteady on my feet, and san k onto it.

He rummaged in a pack and pulled out a foil pouch of . . . something. Beef stroganoff, I think. Maybe it was chicken stir-fry that first day. Huh . . . I don't actually remember what I ate. I remember opening the packet and feeling it warm in my hands. I remember the steam and my stomach rumbling in response to the savory aroma, but that's it. I guess I was so focused on him that I just didn't register what I actually ate.

He did NOT take his mask off. He must have eaten at some point, maybe carried the food into the woods where I wouldn't see, or waited until after I was asleep. That's when he claimed to have eaten that first time, while I was unconscious.

"How long was that, anyway?"

"About four hours. Give or take."

"That's longer than the deer were asleep."

"Yeah . . . Sorry about that." I got the sense he was leaving something out. Like maybe that he'd hit me with a deer-sized dose and it was lucky I wasn't dead. I figured that out later. Not that he ever said it, but I watched him recalibrate doses at th e little camp table later, so it must have been a real issue.

If you've been paying attention, you know he lied about how long I was unconscious. It had been about ten in the morning when I saw him. Four hours would have put it at about two in the afternoon. Maybe three. The light inditated that it was about seven in the evening. I'd actually been asleep for nearly a day and a half. It was, indeed, lucky I hadn't been killed when he shot me. I'm still not certain why his i-Sys didn't flag the weight differential.

If you expect me to tell you what happened during that time, I hate to break it to you, but I don't know.

And yes, I had to pee. Forgive me for not getting into the details of that. Suffice to say that he let me go behind a bush, but he made it very clear that running would be a poor choice. The rifle by the table was an ample reminder. I might have been useful, but I was willing to bet that onlly extended so far. I mean . . . he hadn't planned on kidnapping me in the forest when he saw me. I'd been a surprise addition to whatever he was doing with the deer—which is, I expect, what you really want to know about.

I figure the bidding on this went so high because you are trying to figure out what is causing the deer die-off and wonder if I know. Or if something I saw will make it clear.

I don't know.

I guess I'll just keep typing and hope you read something that makes sense to you, because it sure as hell doesn't make sense to me. That first day, I ate my hot meal of whatever it was, drank my water, and watched him.

"What are you doing?"

"I'm trying to work." But as he said that, his eyes crinkled as if he was grinning under the mask. I think he was taking a certain amount of pleasure in being obstinate. In fact, I'm sure of it based on—doesn't matter. The point is, it looked as if he was smiling, so I kept pushing.

"More things with the deer?"

He shook his head with a little eye roll. Note: That meant he was accessing a datastream.

"Does shaking your head mean 'not things with the deer' or that you won't answer me?"

"Whichever you'd like." He stared into the distance for a moment, clearly reading something off a virteo projection, then blinked it closed and picked up a card with what looked like little black seeds on it. He fed that into the hard-case computer.

"I'd prefer it to mean 'not things with the deer, and I am willing to answer questions.'"

That got the smile again, and the cloth in front of his

mask puffed away a little, as if he'd laughed.

"Do you have a name?"

"Yep."

I waited, scratching an itch on my arm. Oh . . . but he did like playing with me. "What is it?"

"Not going to tell you."

"Oh, come on. I have to call you something."

"Why?" He peered over the edge of the mask at me, sort of the way you see professors look over the edge of their glasses in old movies.

"I can't just say 'Hey, you.'"

"There's just two of us. It's not like I won't know you're talking to me."

"When I think about you, I don't want to just be saying 'the guy' or 'that bastard' all the time in my own head. I mean, if you want me to pick out a name for you . . ."

He laughed outright then. It was surprisingly melodious, as if he laughed up three steps on a scale. "Fine. Call me Johnny."

"Not your real name, I take it?"

"No, but it amuses me." His smile peeked over the edge of the mask. "Though bastard would be fine too."

I grinned at that, and I remembered it felt good to smile. Then I felt ill, because I'm pretty sure that's how Stockholm syndrome starts. Your captor makes you laugh with them an d forget for a second that you're a prisoner. My actual job was not to feel cozy, but to figure out why I was here. That meant asking questions.

"Was the deer okay, Johnny? The one you were waiting on to wake up?"

"Yes." He hesitated and then, miracle of miracles, volunteered more. Maybe making him laugh had been useful after all. "Sometimes they try to stand too soon. I like to make sure they don't fall and hurt themselves."

"They let you get close enough to do that?"

"If they're drugged and I'm there when they wake up, yes."

"But you were away because of me."

Johnny nodded, and his brows pinched together a little. So now I knew he'd done this thing with the deer, whatever it was, more than once. I mean, tha t was sort of clear from how practiced he was with the injector, but the fact that he talked about other times that he'd waited for the deer to awaken made it seem as if this was a regular thing. I picked ato ne of the scabs on my leg, where the bushes had scratched me.

"Was it a problem? Getting back to it?"

"Him. The buck didn't fall, and he spooked as soon as I got close. The doe was fine. Business as usual there."

I want to really point that out. He said, "Business as usual . . ." So here's the question: Why was he so concerned about the health of the deer if whatever he was doing was responsible for the decline in population?

He kept working, and I started paying a little more attention to what he was actually doing.

Again, this is a composite memory. I saw him do this a couple of different times while I was in the woods. The little card with seeds was a blister pack of nanodrives. He fed them into the hard-case machine and programmed them with . . . something. What's significant here is that the machine was NOT connected to the net in any way. I learned that later. So, he had something totally freestanding, and he was programming these little nanodrives. After he got a group of twenty done, he loaded them into the injector gun. I think, in the time I saw him, he did maybe two hundred of these drives.I imagine you have the same questions I did. Why was he injecting the deer with nanodrives? I didn't expect him to answer that, but I was hoping I could figure it out. That evening I let him work for a while, being quiet as if I were compliant. When he stretched at one point, leaning back on the stump to crack his spine, I took a small chance.

I asked him if I could help.

He lowered his hands from his stretch and turned to look at me. His gaze, full bore, is intense and more than a little disturbing. "No."

"I'm handy with tools . . ."

"No. I can be clearer, if you need that, but the answer

is no."

"That from your bosses?"

"That's from me." He turned back to the table and resumed feeding the card back into the hard-case computer. "To anticipate your next 'why,' it's because you are not as sly as you think you are. I'd be an idiot to let you handle any of this."

And THAT made it imperative for me to do just that. "Oh, come on... I'm an Authenticities dealer. I do restoration and repair of antiques. I don't know squat about whatever it is you're doing with the deer—or not with the deer—but I'm good with my hands. And if you're planning on keeping me until you finish whatever it is you're doing, it's in my best interest to make sure you do it faster."

That sounded much better in my head when I said it than it does now. Here, it's so clearly a pose—and a stupid one at that—I'm surprised I don't have a memory of him laughing again.

He just didn't answer. Didn't even acknowledge I'd said anything. Just kept doing stuff with the monitor and the cards as if I weren't in the clearing. And that was the way we passed the rest of the evening. Eventually, it got dark. He told me to go to bed. I did.

I planned on getting up to see if I could find anything useful, but I passed out as soon as my head touched the ground. I blame the lingering drugs in my system.

———————

Dawn woke me.

If you haven't spent the night in the woods, just know that little birdsa re damn noisy. I mean . . . holy shit. They are so loud. And deeply, hatefully,cheerful. Each Disney princess should have made it her mission in life to teach birds to be quiet in the morning. At no point during the three days I was in the woods did I get used to it.

The tent confused me again, but no t as long this time. On the off chance that Johnny was asleep and I could sneak away, I rolled over and pulled the flap of the tent open.

No luck. Johnny was stretched out on the ground in front of the tent. His eyes were open, and he was staring right at me. And yes, he still had that mask on. I didn't get the sense that he'd hurriedly put it back in place either. I flinched a little, but not as badly as earlier.

"I have to pee." My voice was shockingly loud in the clearing, even with the birds in a full frenzy of happiness.

"So do it."

He didn't even lift his head from the rolled-up coat he was using as a pillow. He was in a sleeping bag, but the side was unzipped and one foot hung out. He'd taken his boots off, but otherwise he seemed to be fully dressed.

"Aren't you worried I'll escape?"

"Nope."

"I thought that was why you tranqed me."

"Oh, you might run, but I'm not worried about you ESCAPING."

The hell of it was that he didn't have a reason to be worried about that. Shit. My earlier attempt had shown that, and, thank you, I did not want to get druggged again. I crawled out of the tent, half tempted to knee him as I did. Pretty sure I knew how that would play out, so I didn't even try.

When I got back from peeing he was up, boots on, and rolling up his sleeping bag.

"So what's the plan for today?"

Crouching on his haunches, he glanced up at me, continuing to roll up the sleeping bag. "I'm going out to shoot some things. You're going to stay here."

"That sounds like a long, boring day for me." Though what I was actually thinking was that it would be a chance to look at the stuff he was using.

"So wander around the woods. I'll find you when I get back."

"You're awfully confident in your tracking skills."

He tossed the sleeping bag into the tent and stood. His gaze drifted over to my left, and he tilted his head, listening to something I couldn't hear, and then he repeated someone else's words. "Katya . . . You need to understand that we can find you anywhere now. Please do not cause difficulties. It would be unpleasant."

I have played that over in my head so many times. "We can find you anywhere." And then that extra word. "Now." We can find you anywhere NOW.

They had tagged me.

While I was asleep, he'd inserted a fucking transponder into my body somewhere. Which one of teh scrapes and scratches on my legs and arms wasn't from the woods? Somewhere on my body was an insertion wound. Just a puncture mark large enough to insert a nanodrive like the ones he'd put into the deer. And there was no way for me to know where. If he was smart, it was somewhere on my back where I wouldn't even be able to see it.

It makes me feel sick, thinking about it. I mean, wouldn't you, if someone had inserted something into you without your permission, without your knowledge?

And here's the real brainfuck.

I never found it.

When I got out of the woods, I was taken straight to a hospital. There was no sign of any undocumented foreign matter in my body. My UV tattoos, sure. Dermal implants, fillings, onboard battery storage, my i-Sys connections, all the other little things we modify ourselves with—those show up just fine, but no one found anything that wasn't already in my records. So the question I keep asking is: Was he bluffing then, and I never had a transponder? Or did he mask it with one of the otehr artifacts already in my body?

He could be watching me type this.

Creepy as hell, huh?

Try living with the idea. Yeah... I don't enjoy it either.

Or maybe he really was just bluffing, and I could have walked out of that forest at any time, which is its own brand of creepy. Because that means he was using my own mind and nothing else to hold me. Either way, it's unpleasant, and I could spend a lifetime second-guessing myself like that.

At the time, I just cursed at him. I don't even remember what I said; I was just so sick and angry that I ranted at him and called him half a dozen names, most of them more than once. Above the mask, his eyes were impassive. He didn't flinch; he didn't smile. He just bore witness to my rage. And I'll give him that. He didn't ignore me and go back to work; he waited until I'd wound down and run out of things to call him and whoever the fuck his bosses were.

I stood there, shaking with anger, thinking again

about how I'd been washed while I was asleep and imagining every possible violation. He looked down then, and I realized he was not as impassive as I'd thought. His hands were gripped into fists. He stretched the fingers out slowly, as if working the tension out of them. I am not certain—I might just be projecting this onto him—but I think he was not happy about having tagged me.

Without a word, he turned and walked across the clearing to his bag. He pulled it open and rummaged inside for a bit before pulling out a book. A paper book, mind you, not a reader. He set it on the table and all he said was, "If you get bored."

The crazy thing—I mean the part that really makes me question my own mind—is that my first instinct was to take a Capture so that later I would have the provenance of the book, in case it was something I could put up for sale. How stupid is that?

He slung the rifle over his shoulder, strapped teh small kit to his belt, and strode off into the forest.

I spent the day trying to break into the cases where he stowed everything—and failing, because they were print-sealed and would, presumably, only open to him. Likewise, the robo-mule would not turn on—not that it would have been a terribly useful thing to have, since I could walk as fast as one of those in the woods, and they weren't exactly stealthy. Great for packing gear though.

Periodically, the forest would echo with the sound of the rifle. Sometimes one shot, then nothing for an hour. Sometimes four or five shots, clustered together. I had walked away from the clearing, but I started to worry that a) I would wander into the range of gunfire or that b) I wouldn't be able to find my way back before Johnny returned.

I wouldn't want him to think I had tried to run away again, would I? I actually considered that. Can you imagine?

The book. You'll want to know about that. I did eventually pick it up, and yes, I read it, because I was bored. It was a third edition of Bashar's book, A SYMMETRY FRAMED, fourth printing. Coffee stain on page 218 means that its owner had probably stayed up late reading. Pencil marks under key sentences such as "True power lies in positioning the fulcrum of events, not in grasping them by the lever," and "Western capitalism was always unable to account for either the costs or benefits of naturally occurring systems, instead treating them only as inputs to human-designed industrial and economic processes."

The bottom of the book's cover had been gnawed on by a puppy, much like the dictionary.

Of course, I'd need to get it into a lab and show it to an AI to be certain, but I never had that opportunity with this particular artifact. It's too bad, really, because it was loaded with wabi-sabi.

Johnny came back in the evening, his gun slung over his shoulder. As usual, I didn't hear him coming. One moment, I was alone in the clearing; the next, he was stepping out of the trees. Again, I jumped.

"Would you STOP doing that?"

"What?" He paused in the act of slinging the rifle off his shoulder and looked genuinely baffled.

"Most people make noise when they walk. You're like a freaking ghost."

"Ah." His motion continued as if I hadn't stopped him. "Apologies. Habits die hard, and silence is more useful in the woods than noise."

"Well, I'm getting tired of being frightened." And that was true in more ways than one. The book might have helped me clarify my own position. It might have been a mistake, in fact, for him to give it to me. Bashar was very good at explaining how to use what power you had to achieve your goals. I was over halfway through teh book by then, past the place where the coffee stain was.

"Again, I apologize. I'll make noise when I come back tomorrow."

"Tomorrow. We're still going to be in these woods tomorrow?"

"Probably for the rest of the week." He pulled the clip

from the rifle and checked the chamber before he leaned the gun against the table.

"That many deer?"

"Yes." He thumbed opened one of the cases. Inside were rows of ammunition nestled in foam. He slid the clip into its place and shut the case again. I could hear the slight SNICK as it sealed.

"Johnny, I need you to explain to me what I have to do with deer and why you are keeping me here."

"Or?"

"Or I won't cooperate when we get to whatever it is your bosses want me to do."

"We don't need you to cooperate."

That stopped me. And chilled me.

"You were in the way when I had work to do. I need you to be quiet about what you saw until I'm finished. My choices were to bring you with me, or to kill you." He cocked his head and glanced to the left at his bosses, whoever they were, in his virteo projection. He shook his head, I think at them. "I took responsibility for you, but this has nothing to do with you."

"But . . . but you said we had something to discuss. My client list interested you"

He stared, and the sun seemed to drop visibly lower in the sky while he thought. Then he shook his head.

"Oh, come on."

"Have you eaten dinner?"

"You can't just change the subject"

"Yes I can. You know I can. Do you want something to eat?"

"Bastard."

"See. I was right. I told you I didn't need a name."

I did not give him the courtesy of a laugh. I sulked, like a goddamn five-year-old. I sat down in the only chair and picked up his goddamn book and started to read. Then realized that it was HIS book, and I wanted to throw the thing across the clearing, but I didn't because that would have done exactly no good. Nothing, in fact, that I could do would do any good at all. The utter impotence of my situation—the helplessness of knowing there were no good choices . . . The only one open to me, to wait, seemed like a surrender.

He gave me a foil pouch of some other unmemorable meal. I'd had dried fruit and a trail bar for breakfast, a different forgettable pouch for lunch. Johnny still didn't eat in front of me. Oh, no. That would have meant removing his mask, and that might have revealed who he was.

Silent, resentful, I went to bed when full dark came. That night I didn't sleep well at all.

Despite that, the birds woke me again at dawn. I lay in the tent, glaring at the roof. If I could have killed them with my mind, I would have. Alas, the cheerful little bastards lived on.

The inside of my mouth tasted as if something had died in it. Modern advances are all well and good for making sure your dental hygiene is in good order, but when you go days without brushing your teeth, there's a bit of a buildup there. My breath stank. I stank. I'd been wearing the same clothes for days now.

I crawled out of the tent hating everything and everyone.

Johnny was awake, watching me again. I didn't jump this time.

"I need some clean clothes."

"Good morning." He sat up. "I haven't got any to give you."

I was so frustrated that the state of my clothes mattered more than it should have. "Is there a stream where I can wash them?"

"They'll be wet all day. Not enough sun to dry."

I asked him again. "Is there. A stream. Where I can wash them?"

He rolled his eyes, and I just barely bit back a scream of frustration—and only then because in the dawn light the glow of his virteo projection was a little more visible.

"Yes. There's a stream about a half hour walk due east. There's a bank closer, but walking due east will make it easier to find your way back."

"If I get lost, you can always come find me."

He blinked the virteo off. "I can."

"You're shooting things again today?"

"Yes."

"Try not to shoot me."

He sighed and got out of the sleeping bag. "Believe it or not, Katya, that's been the goal all along."

I grabbed some dried fruit from his bag and stalked off toward the rising sun to wash my damn clothes.

To you, now, I will admit that this was a mistake. It left me with wet clothes in the early morning, and a walk back through the woods with the choice of either wearing said wet clothes, or adding scratches to my torso to my list of injuries. I opted to wear them. The technical fabric was good at wicking water away, though not in those volumes. Still, that was something, and they dried fast enough that by lunchtime I was only mildly damp. The gunfire that day had been mostly west of me. It stopped shortly after lunch, I think. I remember getting to the end of Bashar's chapter on "self-actualizing inter-penetrated communities" and realizing that I hadn't heard anything for hours. Then I wenton to the next chapter.

In all other ways, the day was exactly the same as the one previous, with one exception.

I was sitting in my chair when I heard a slight rustle of leaves at the edge of the clearing. A deer stepped out of the woods. A buck. He lifted his head, under the crown of antlers, and his nostrils flared. Those delicate, velvet ears flicked back, listening to something behind him. He turned his head and regarded me. I sat, utterly frozen, in my chair. I fully expected Johnny to shoot the deer, but the woods stayed quiet around us. After a moment, evidently deciding I was not a threat, the deer crossed through the clearing. A few paces behind him, a collection of does and a younger buck trailed behind. I wondered if they had been tagged yet with Johnny's nanodrives.

In a few breaths, they were gone again, as if they had never been. I sagged in my chair and went back to waiting. I was so tired from my anger the previous night that I half dozed. I could be poetic here and say that I dreamed of deer, since no one can contradict me, but the truth is that if I dreamed, I don't remember it.

I awoke with a crick in my neck. I hate those.

When I heard the footsteps in the woods, even as far away as they were, I was surprised, then pleased that Johnny had remembered my request not to frighten me. He made a tremendous crashing, compared to his previous progress. I stood, rubbing the ache in my neck, and picked A SYMMETRY FRAMED up from where it had fallen. The slight brown discoloration in the corner had added my own bit of decay to the book, though I'm not sure anything about my nap was graceful.

I can't say exactly what made me realize something was wrong. I think it was that his footsteps were so irregular. A set of five, rushed together, then a pause before another syncopated series of footsteps. There was a moment when I thought it wasn't going to be Johnny at all, and I didn't know if that would be good or not.When I caught sight of him, his camouflage made it difficult to make out his figure when he was at rest, but the erratic, weaving motion throu gh the trunks pulled at my eye.

And then I saw the blood.

In a forest made of browns and greens, blood is shockingly, artificially red.

There is something about the sight of blood that makes me run toward someone to help, even someone I have good reason to hate.

I ran toward Johnny. He had stopped to lean against a tree. This was what had made his progress through the forest so staggering and uneven. He was barely on his feet at all. The front of his shirt was stained a deep red, shading to brown and, in places, almost black. He had a hand pressed against his stomach, and his fingers were caked with blood.

"What happened?"

His voice was cracked and hollow. "Deer. Woke up angry."

I slipped an arm around him, and he let me. The rifle was slung over his back, and his handgun was at his waist. I could have taken either and fled, leaving him there. But I also couldn't have.

He let me take some of his weight, and we walked the last yards back to the camp. I eased him down into the chair. "Do you have a first-aid kit?"

"Second trunk from the bottom." He gestured in that general direction and beckoned. "It's keyed to me."

I shoved off the other trunks and picked it up. The thing weighed more than I expected, and I staggered a little as I carried it to him. At his side, I dropped it with a thump. He bent forward to reach the print reader and toppled out of the chair. I reached for him, but my hands just brushed his coat. He hit the ground.

Johnny grunted at the impact and tensed, his whole body freezing.

By that point, I had knelt next to him and had my hands on his back. "What can I do?"

He shook his head. Let his breath out. Tried to push up to his knees, but he was clearly spent. I helped him roll over instead. As he did, the damage was clearer. The deer had stabbed—no, wait. There's a word for this, isn't there? The deer had GORED him with its antlers. A rip in the cloth of his shirt was mirrored in his skin. I could see parts of his body you're not supposed to see. I didn't understand how he'd managed to walk back. Oh—and here's the really insane thing. He still had the mask on.

I dragged the case close enough that he could thumb it open. The seal gave with a hiss, and I opened the case to root through it. There was nothing I could imagine that would be able to deal with his horrific wound. "We need to get you to a hospital."

"Not sure that's an option."

He clearly couldn't walk out of here, and there was no way I could carry him. I cut his shirt out of the way and pressed a nu-derm pad against his stomach. It sealed against the skin, controlling the bleeding, but would do little to keep him alive beyond that. I had this crazy thought about making a litter out of the sleeping bag and trying to drag him out of the forest. As I turned to look for sticks, I saw the robo-mule. "I can strap you to that."

He stared at me and then at it. "Okay. Yes. Thank you."

"Can you key it to me?"

"Yes." He pointed to the cases again. "Grab the blue one and bring it to me."

That one was where he'd put the hard-body computer the other night. I grabbed the case. He opened it. To my surprise, he didn't do anything with the computer; instead, he pulled out my earbud. "Once you get me on the robo-mule, start walking north. You should hit a road in a couple of hours."

Surely he didn't have a couple of hours. "I can't just leave you."

"Ah . . . but you have to get out of range to call for help."

"Out of range of what?"

"Me and the d—my damper."

I don't know, but I think he almost said "the deer." I didn't question him and probably should have, since I think his judgment was slipping. Seeing someone dying though . . .

I pointed at the hard-body computer. "Can't I just call out on that?"

"Local network only. Gotta hoof it." He held up his hand. "Help me up?"

I got him to his feet and over to the robo-mule. We used the straps from the tent to improvise reins that he could grip. I used the luggage tie-downs to create a harness that would hold him on if he lost consciousness. We both thought that was pretty likely, all things considered. Apparently, he'd passed out on the way back to the camp. I had no idea how he was still alive. His breathing was pretty ragged by the time I was finished with the tie-downs.

I told him he should take the mask off.

He shook his head and tugged it higher on his face. "Got an NDA, and right now I really need my employer to stay invested."

"Surely they would understand—"

Again he shook his head, stopping my protest with a gesture. "Not the sort that understands things like breathing difficulties."

You hear what he wasn't saying? He couldn't come out and say he was working for a nonhuman entity, but I think that was what he meant. Whether it was an AI or a corporation, I don't know. But whatever he was do-ing with the deer, they didn't want it traced back to them, and that meant keeping Johnny unidentifiable.

I should have thought of that, I really should have, be-fore I left him.

We got the robo-mule going, and once it was aimed and keyed to head north, I set out. At first, I was still close enough to hear it clomping through the woods, gy-ros whirring; then I left them behind. He'd said a couple of hours, and I was determined to try to get out of range as fast as possible. Every few minutes, I'd query to see if Lizzie was there. Not a thing. This surprised me, because I'd thought my data connection earlier had cut off when Johnny was close to me. I didn't realize the range. So my calves and thighs ached from the pace I was setting. The forest added a whole new set of scratches to my growing collection. Too bad I can't sell those as a unique experience . . .

"Katya!" The call from Lizzie nearly dropped me in my tracks as all my systems came back online at once. One minute I was out of range; the next minute the full connectivity of my life slammed back into me. Messages, calendar alerts, namedrops, interest points—all of it flooding back in to demand my attention. I shook it all away and focused on Lizzie.

"Here. Do you have me? I need emergency services."

"Yes. Yes, I have you. Where have you been? How are you injured?" The i-Sys almost sounded concerned.

"I'm not injured—well, not seriously, but someone else is."

"Show me the injury, and I will have a medical patch assess it."

"I'm not with him. Send the emergency team to me, and then I'll lead them to where he is." With that, I realized I would need to keep walking north until they got a lock on me, or Johnny would catch up and I'd get cut off again. "Please hurry. He's lost a lot of blood and was stabbed. Sort of."

"Complying. Emergency medical service is en route. Please be advised that this will be billed to your account if the patient is unable or unwilling to cover the charges."

"I understand."

They were fast. Fifteen minutes after the call, during which time I made an attempt to answer the messages that Lizzie rated as urgent priority, a medchopper disturbed the forest with its rotors.

From here, you can watch the public record of what happened, and I'm assuming you have. My cameras were working again. The medteam had their LiveConnects running the entire time.

You can see the way they reacted to me, and the blood that covered me. I hadn't realized how stained my clothes had become with Johnny's blood.

Once I reassured them, we retraced my steps. We got all the way back to the clearing. No Johnny. No robo-mule. The site was completely empty, and the ground had been churned by the hooves of deer. No trace of humans at all.

The only thing that makes my story at all believable is that I was offline for three days. During that time I had moved from south of Salem northward by about 400 miles, close to Lake Chelan. The bike and cart were where I had said they were hidden, but I could have done that myself. And since mine were the only footprints the investigators found . . . well. It's easy to see how it might have been a publicity stunt designed to raise the price on my merchandise by giving it a unique provenance.

But the blood—that should be proof, shouldn't it?

It was blood from a deer.

I REMEMBER seeing the ragged hole in his stomach and innards. I remember how gray his skin looked and how labored his breathing was. But those memories ... they must be false, right? Something I THOUGHT I saw in the moment. Something that took advantage of the failability of memory.

And why? That's what is hard to understand. Why would he fake an injury or a death if all he had to do was let me go? And even then, why not use human blood from a blood bank?

I have wondered ... It has occurred to me that it might have been a message. Though that raises its own set of questions.

I looked for him.

After everyone had left, I went back into the woods. I remember standing by a stream and having Lizzie's voice cut off. A deer stepped out of the trees and bent down to drink. Nothing else stirred except the water and the leaves. After a moment, the deer lifted its head, leaped across the stream, and faded back into the trees. A few minutes later, Lizzie's voice came back as if we hadn't stopped talking.

I don't know if Johnny lived, or what exactly he was

doing with the deer. I don't know what his plans were for me. If you had been hoping that I could give you answers to the deer die-off, I'm sorry that I can't. I don't even know what happened to me.

I know that's frustrating for you, so let me offer you the questions I've been asking myself.

Have you been in the forest? Have you seen deer corpses? Or have you relied on what the net tells you about the die-off?

Because I don't think the deer are dying, I think they're being taken offline, and the nanodrives they were injected with establish a nonhuman network. Changing the deer themselves wouldn't be enough though, because the smart dust in the region would still report them, right?

Unless those nanodrives are rewriting everything the deer comes in contact with. I've asked about that. It's possible, and in a lot of ways it makes the fact that Johnny needed to tranquilize them make more sense. A transmitter—he could have just injected that from a distance. But if he needed time to make sure their systems recalibrated before releasing them . . . well.

But that's just a guess. It's like Bashar says in A SYMMETRY FRAMED—"The land has an unwilling connection to us."

It makes you wonder doesn't it?

I was unconscious for over twenty-four hours, which is plenty of time to recalibrate someone's system. With the client list I have, what would happen if I were released into the wild like the deer?

What would happen if I were made an object of curiosity to attract a specific client?

And my last question: What if they're looking for you? Or people LIKE you?

This typewriter is covered in dust. It's part of its wabi-sabi. If the smart dust around me is mbeing rewritten, what about the dust ont his typweriter? The dust around you?

Has your connection to the net dropped recently?

That's got you wondering, I expect . . . Think of it as a bonus with your purchase. I've given you the gift of uncertainty.

About the Author

Author photograph © 2012 Rod Searcey

MARY ROBINETTE KOWAL is the author of The Glamourist Histories series of fantasy novels. She has received the Campbell Award for Best New Writer, three Hugo Awards, and two *RT Book Reviews* Reviewer's Choice Award for Best Fantasy Novel. Her work has been a finalist for the Hugo, Nebula, and Locus Awards. Her stories have appeared in *Strange Horizons, Asimov's Science Fiction and Fact,* and several Year's Best anthologies as well as in her collection *Scenting the Dark and Other Stories* from Subterranean Press.

A professional puppeteer and voice actor, Mary founded Other Hand Productions and has performed for *LazyTown* (CBS), the Center for Puppetry Arts, and

Jim Henson Pictures. Her designs have garnered two UNIMA-USA Citations of Excellence, the highest award an American puppeteer can achieve. She also records fiction for authors such as Kage Baker, Cory Doctorow, and John Scalzi.

Mary lives in Chicago with her husband, Rob, and over a dozen manual typewriters.

Visit maryrobinettekowal.com.

TOR·COM

Science fiction. Fantasy. The universe.

And related subjects.

*

More than just a publisher's website, *Tor.com*
is a venue for **original fiction, comics,** and
discussion of the entire field of SF and fantasy,
in all media and from all sources. Visit our site
today—and join the conversation yourself.